PZ8.3.R2325 T54 2004

Ravishankar, Anushka.

Tiger on a tree /

2004.

2005 10 06

P9-DOA-466

Tiger
on a Tree

Anushka Ravishankar

Pulak Biswas

170201

SENECA WITHDRAWN COLLEGE LIBRARY

Farrar, Straus and Giroux
New York

Tiger, tiger

on the shore

Does he want

to go across?

Make a dash?

Be bold? Be rash?

splash!

Tiger, tiger,

going far

Baaaaaaaa

Yaaaaaaa

aaah!

This tree is the

only place to be!

Tiger! Tiger?

On a tree!

Tiger? On a tree?

Rubbish! Cannot be!

It's true! I saw it too! Now what to do?

Get him! Net him!

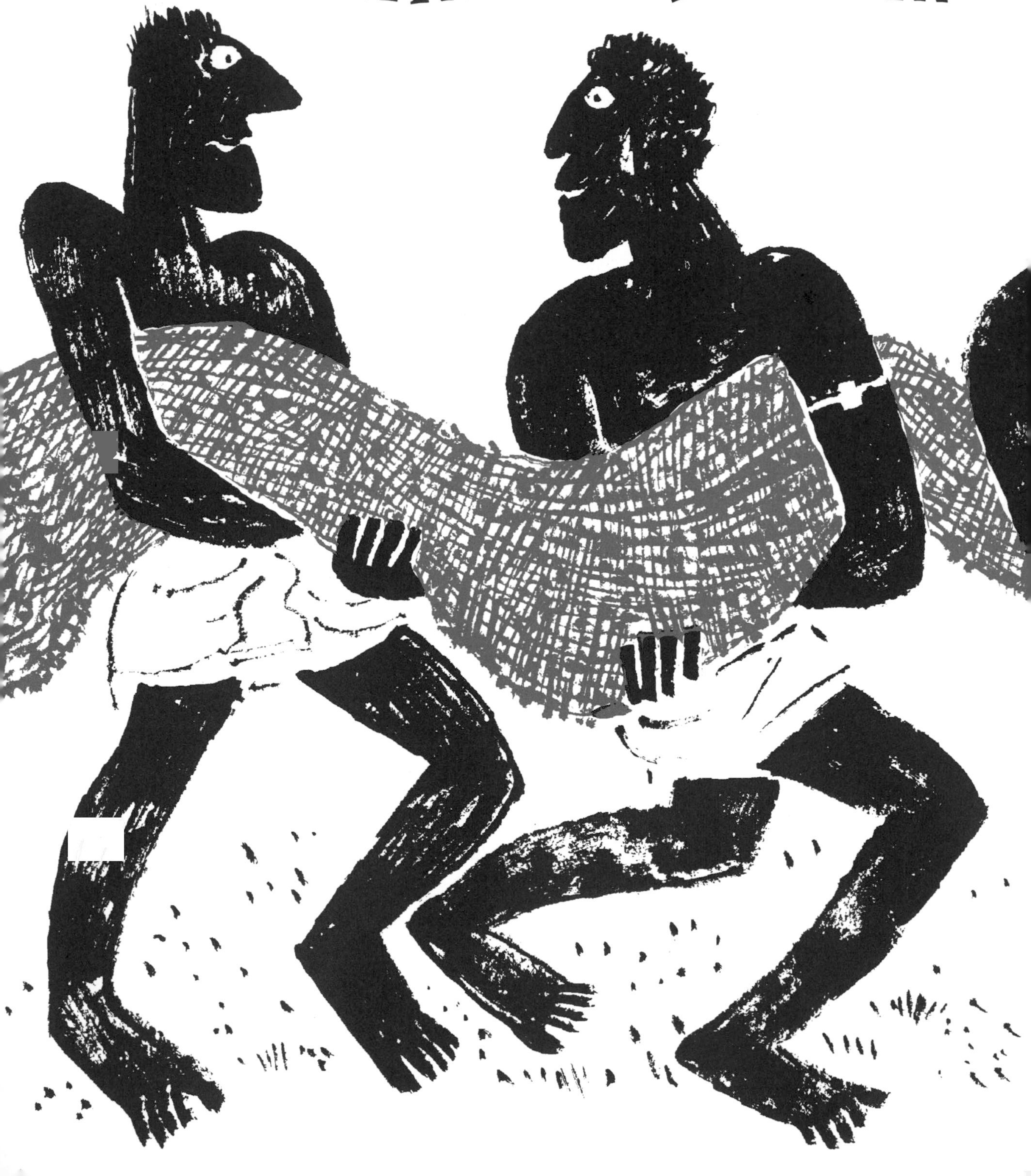

He might!

Shoo him!

Boo him!

Make him jump!

Dum duma dum dum dum

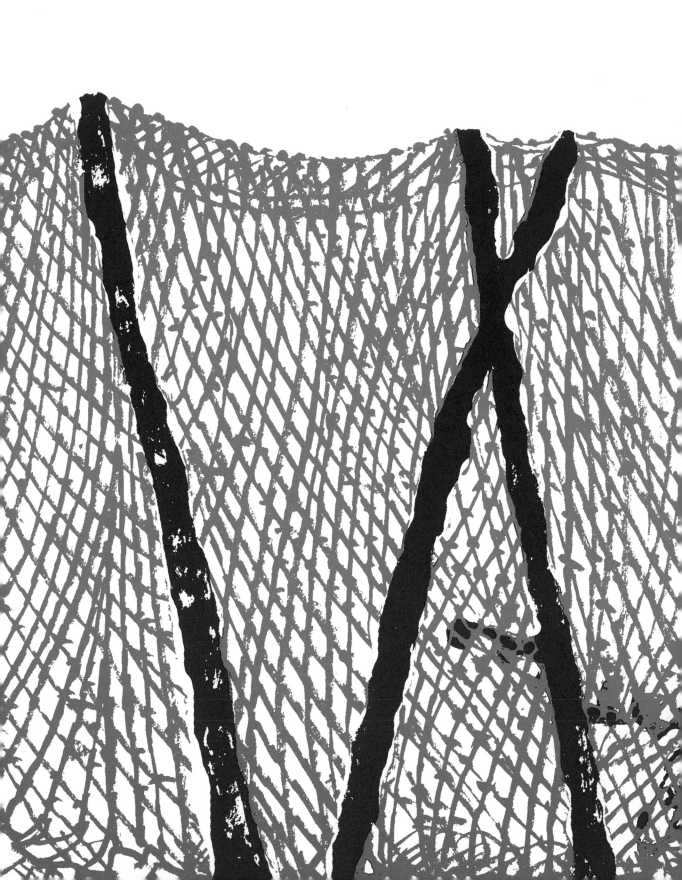

Thump.

He's caught.

He's got.

Now what?

Stick him up with glue?

Paint him an electric blue?

I know, set him free.

Free???

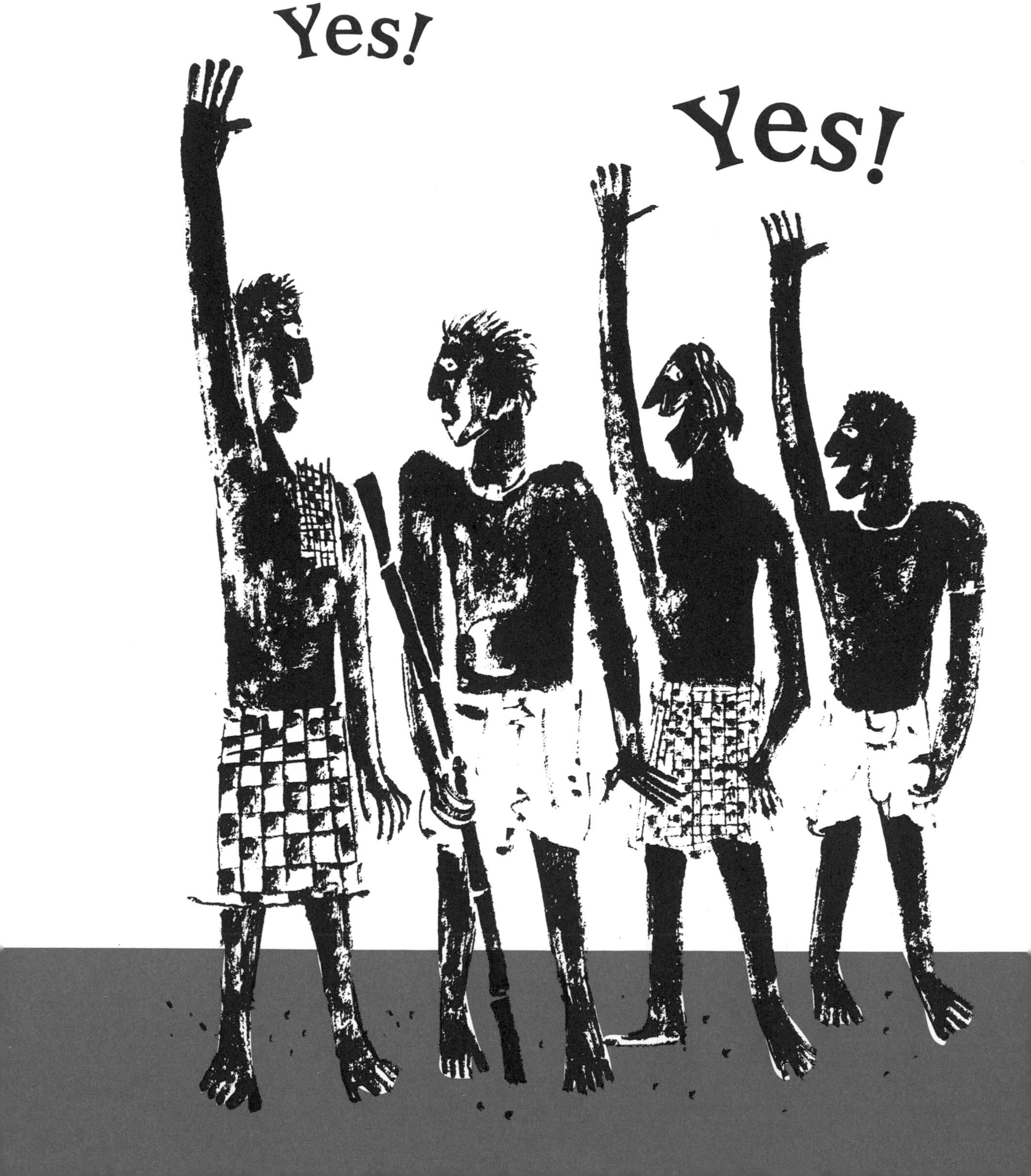
Yes!
Yes!

So.

Tiger, tiger on the shore

Copyright © 1997 by Tara Publishing
All rights reserved
Distributed in Canada by Douglas & McIntyre Ltd.
Printed and bound in the United States of America by Berryville Graphics
Originally published in 1997 by Tara Publishing, Chennai, India, www.tarabooks.com
First American edition, 2004
1 3 5 7 9 10 8 6 4 2

www.fsgkidsbooks.com

Library of Congress Cataloging-in-Publication Data
Ravishankar, Anushka.
    Tiger on a tree / Anushka Ravishankar ; pictures by Pulak Biswas.— 1st American ed.
        p. cm.
    Summary: After trapping a tiger in a tree, a group of men must decide what to do with it.
    ISBN 0-374-37555-0
    [1. Tigers—Fiction.   2. Stories in rhyme.]   I. Biswas, Pulak, ill.

PZ8.3.R2325 Ti 2004
[E]—dc21

                                                                          2003049050

WITHDRAWN

NEWNHAM
COLLEGE LIBRARY